BILLY BEG
AND HIS BULL

An Irish Tale retold by Ellin Greene

illustrated by Kimberly Bulcken Root

Holiday House/New York

For Bill, my dragonslayer,
and for Michael and Eric
—E.G.

For Charles and Jane Stephenson Root
—K.B.R.

Ill⌐

⌐ht © 1994 by Ellin Greene
⌐ 1994 by Kimberly Bulcken Root
HTS RESERVED
United States of America
FIRST EDITION

⌐ngress Cataloging-in-Publication Data
Greene, Ellin, 1927–
Billy   ⌐ his bull : an Irish tale / retold by Ellin Greene ;
⌐.⌐strated by Kimberly Bulcken Root. — 1st ed.
          p.   cm.
Summary: With magical gifts from the bull his mother had given
him, the son of an Irish king manages to prove his bravery and
win a princess as his wife.
ISBN 0-8234-1100-1
[1. Fairy tales. 2. Folklore—Ireland.] I. Root, Kimberly
Bulcken, ill. II. Title.
PZ8.G828Bi   1994   93-7730   CIP   AC
            398.21—dc20
                [E]

AUTHOR'S NOTE

"Billy Beg and His Bull" has been a favorite of library story-hour listeners for almost a century. My telling is based on that of the great Irish shanachie, Seumas MacManus (1869–1960), published in his collection, *In Chimney Corners* (Doubleday and McClure, 1899).

In retelling the MacManus version for today's young readers/ listeners, I have tried to retain the cadenced speech and "runs" that are so characteristic of Irish folktales—for example, the description of the fight between Billy Beg's bull and the Black Bull of the Forest: "They knocked the soft ground into hard, and the hard into soft, the soft into spring wells, the spring wells into rocks, and the rocks into high hills."

Incidentally, "beg" or "beag" (Irish spelling) means small, or as we would say, "Little Billy."

As a child growing up in Donegal, MacManus learned the art of storytelling from "the women telling their fairy stories and the old men reciting ancient folktales" around the glow of a peat fire in some Irish cottage. MacManus became a teacher, then a writer and a lecturer on storytelling. He spent winters in America and summers in his beloved Donegal, delighting listeners young and old with his tales. For MacManus, storytelling was always associated with joy, the awakening of the imagination, and a sense of wonder.

—*Ellin Greene*

Once on a time, in olden Ireland, there lived a king and a queen who had one son, and he was called Billy Beg. When Billy was just a wee lad, the queen gave him a little bull calf. Billy was very fond of the bull, and the bull was just as fond of him. The two were never apart.

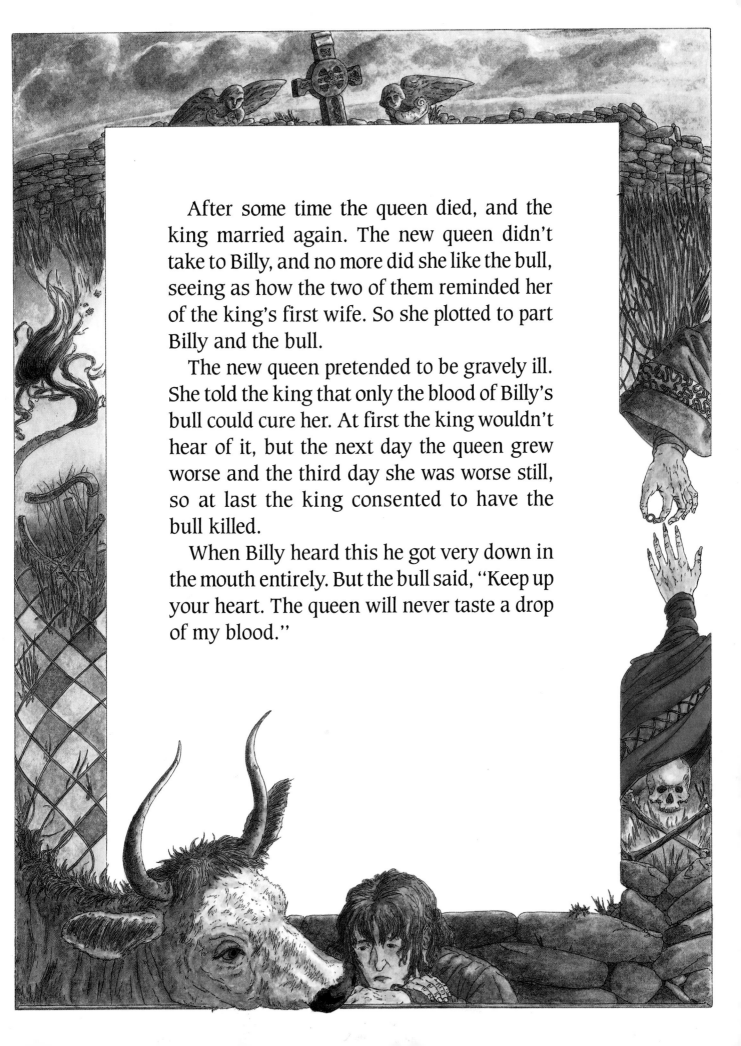

After some time the queen died, and the king married again. The new queen didn't take to Billy, and no more did she like the bull, seeing as how the two of them reminded her of the king's first wife. So she plotted to part Billy and the bull.

The new queen pretended to be gravely ill. She told the king that only the blood of Billy's bull could cure her. At first the king wouldn't hear of it, but the next day the queen grew worse and the third day she was worse still, so at last the king consented to have the bull killed.

When Billy heard this he got very down in the mouth entirely. But the bull said, "Keep up your heart. The queen will never taste a drop of my blood."

The next day the queen got up from her sickbed to see the bull killed. But before the wicked deed could be done, the bull said to Billy, "Jump on my back." Up Billy jumped, and with that the bull leaped nine miles high, nine miles deep, and nine miles broad, and came down with Billy sticking between his horns.

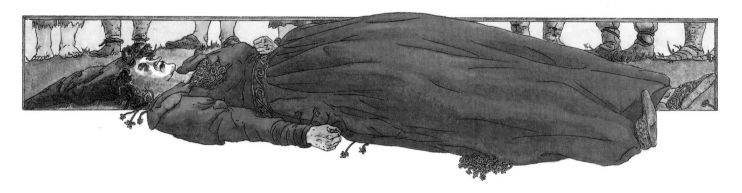

Hundreds were looking on, dazed at the sight, when through the crowd the bull rushed, and right over the queen, killing her dead. Away he galloped where you wouldn't know day by night, nor night by day, over high hills and low hills, farther than I can tell you and you can tell me. At last he stopped.

"Now then," said the bull to Billy, "put your hand in my left ear, and you'll find a napkin. When you spread it out, it will be covered with food and drink fit for the king himself." Billy did this and ate and drank to his heart's content. Then he rolled up the napkin and put it back in the bull's ear.

"Now put your hand in my right ear, and you'll find a stick. If you swing it over your head three times, it will turn into a sword and give you the strength of a thousand men. When you have no more need of it as a sword, it will change back into a stick again." Billy did all this. "Well and good," said the bull. "Now then, Billy, at twelve o'clock tomorrow, I'm to fight a great bull."

Billy and the bull started off and away until they came to a wood where the great bull was waiting. The two bulls fought long and hard, and at last Billy's bull killed the other bull and drank his blood.

Then Billy took the napkin out of the bull's left ear and spread it out and ate a hearty dinner. The bull said to Billy, said he, "At twelve o'clock tomorrow, I'm to meet the brother of the bull I killed today, and we'll have a hard fight."

Billy and the bull started off and away until they came to the wood where the second bull was waiting. The bulls fought long and hard, but at last Billy's bull killed the other bull and drank his blood.

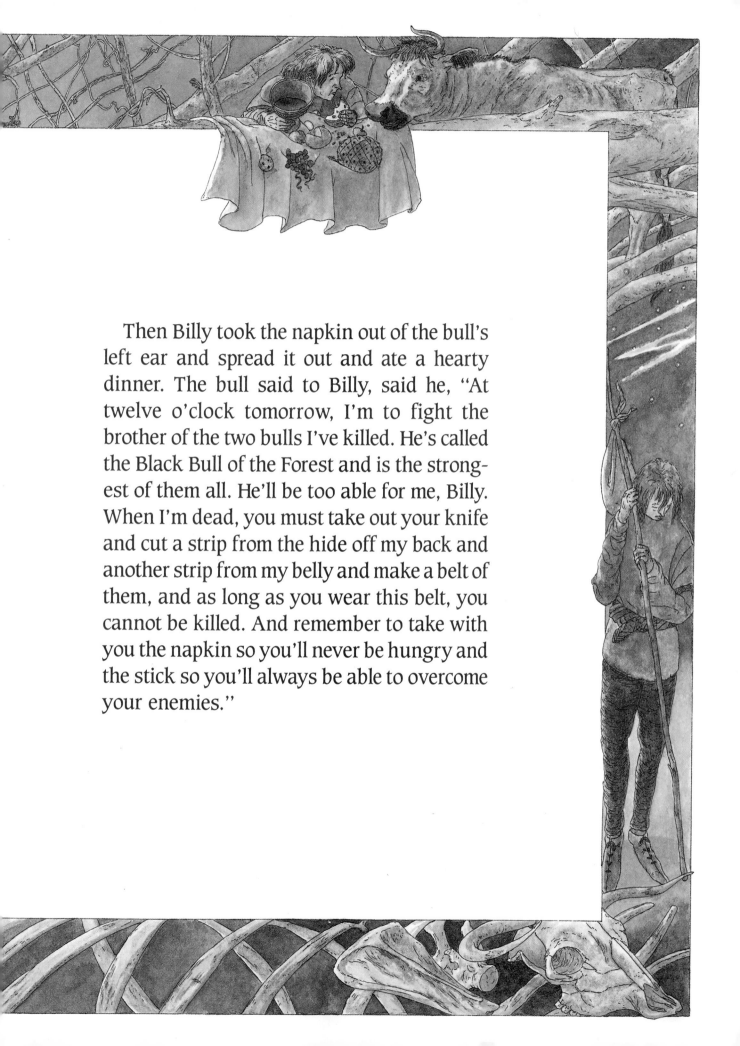

Then Billy took the napkin out of the bull's left ear and spread it out and ate a hearty dinner. The bull said to Billy, said he, "At twelve o'clock tomorrow, I'm to fight the brother of the two bulls I've killed. He's called the Black Bull of the Forest and is the strongest of them all. He'll be too able for me, Billy. When I'm dead, you must take out your knife and cut a strip from the hide off my back and another strip from my belly and make a belt of them, and as long as you wear this belt, you cannot be killed. And remember to take with you the napkin so you'll never be hungry and the stick so you'll always be able to overcome your enemies."

They started off and away and sure enough at twelve o'clock the next day, they met the great Black Bull of the Forest. The two bulls started to fight, and the like of that fight was never seen before nor since. They knocked the soft ground into hard, the hard into soft, the soft into spring wells, the spring wells into rocks, and the rocks into high hills. At last the great Black Bull of the Forest killed Billy's bull and drank his blood.

Billy thought his heart would break. He cried over the bull for two days, neither eating nor drinking. After his fast he was very hungry, so he spread out the napkin and ate a hearty dinner. Then he cut a strip of hide from the bull's back and another from his belly and made a belt for himself. He put the belt on and, taking the napkin and the stick, set off to seek his fortune.

He traveled for three days and three nights until he came to a great house. When Billy asked the master of the house for work, the man said he needed someone to take his cows to pasture. "But," warned the man, "there are three giant brothers who come to steal the milk from the cows every day and kill the boy who's herding them. If you want to try, you can, but we won't fix your wages until you come back alive."

"Agreed then," said Billy.

So the next morning he got up and drove the cows to the orchard. The morning passed quietly, but about midday, Billy heard three terrible roars that shook the apples from the trees, rattled the horns on the cows, and made the hair stand up on Billy's head.

There stood a frightful giant with three heads. "You're too big for one bite and too small for two," said the giant. "What will I do with you?"

"I'll fight you," said Billy, swinging the stick three times over his head. With that, the stick changed into a sword and gave him the strength of a thousand men.

But the giant laughed at the size of Billy. "What way do you prefer to be killed?" he roared. "With a swing by the back or a cut of the sword?"

"With a swing by the back," said Billy.

So they began to wrestle, and Billy lifted the giant clean off the ground. When the giant came down, he sank into the earth up to his armpits. "Spare me," bawled the giant, but with a sweep of his sword, Billy cut off the giant's three heads.

It was evening by this time, so Billy drove the cows home.

"Well," said the master, "this beats me. No herd boy has ever come back alive before. Did you see anything in the orchard, Billy?" he asked.

"Nothing worse than myself," said Billy. "What about my wages now?"

"Well," said the master, "you'll hardly come out of the orchard alive tomorrow, so we'll wait until then."

Next morning after breakfast, Billy drove the cows into the orchard again. He didn't hear anything unusual until about twelve o'clock. Then he heard three terrible roars, twice as loud as the day before, and in came a frightful giant with six heads. The giant raged at Billy for killing his brother and said he would make him pay. "But you're too big for one bite and too small for two," shouted the giant. "What will I do with you?"

"I'll fight you," said Billy, swinging his stick three times over his head and turning it into a sword that gave him the strength of a thousand men.

The giant laughed at the size of him and roared, "What way do you prefer to be killed? With a swing by the back or a cut of the sword?"

"With a swing by the back," said Billy.

They set to, and Billy lifted the giant clean off his feet. When the giant came down, he sank into the earth up to his armpits. "Spare me," he cried, but with a sweep of his sword, Billy cut off the giant's six heads.

It was evening by this time, so Billy drove the cows home.

If the master was surprised to see Billy come back the night before, he was ten times more surprised now. "Did you see anything in the orchard today?" he asked.

"Nothing worse than myself," said Billy. "And now, what about my wages?"

"Never mind about your wages until tomorrow," said the master. "I think you'll hardly come back alive again."

Next morning after breakfast, Billy set off to the orchard with the cows.

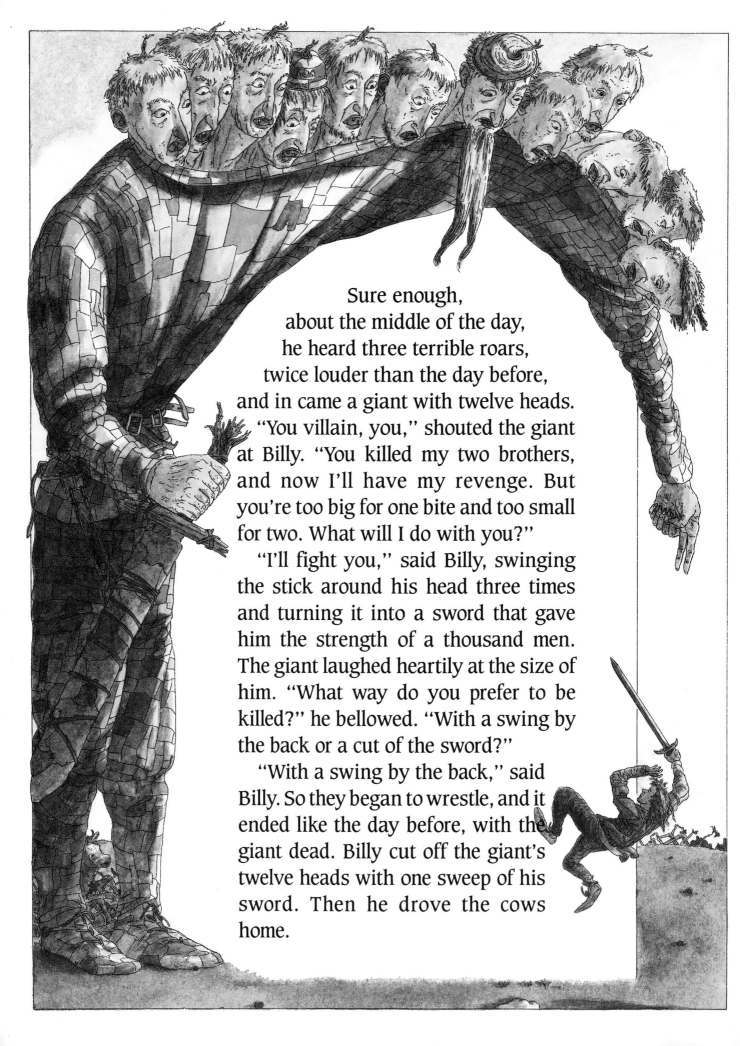

Sure enough,
about the middle of the day,
he heard three terrible roars,
twice louder than the day before,
and in came a giant with twelve heads.
"You villain, you," shouted the giant
at Billy. "You killed my two brothers,
and now I'll have my revenge. But
you're too big for one bite and too small
for two. What will I do with you?"

"I'll fight you," said Billy, swinging
the stick around his head three times
and turning it into a sword that gave
him the strength of a thousand men.
The giant laughed heartily at the size of
him. "What way do you prefer to be
killed?" he bellowed. "With a swing by
the back or a cut of the sword?"

"With a swing by the back," said
Billy. So they began to wrestle, and it
ended like the day before, with the
giant dead. Billy cut off the giant's
twelve heads with one sweep of his
sword. Then he drove the cows
home.

The master was more surprised than ever to see Billy, and he asked, "Did you see nothing in the orchard today?"

"Nothing worse than myself," said Billy. "And now, what about my wages?"

"You're a good lad, and I'll give you any wages you ask for in the future," said the master.

The next morning the master told Billy that he was going to see a fight and that Billy must stay home and take care of the animals.

"What fight?" asked Billy.

"Why," said the master, "the king's daughter is going to be eaten by a dragon if the greatest fighter in the land doesn't kill the dragon first. But if he's able to kill the dragon, he'll get to marry the princess."

"That will be fine," said Billy.

On the way to the orchard, Billy passed the people going to see the fight. "Aren't you coming?" they asked.

"What would the likes of me be doing there?" Billy replied.

But as soon as they were gone, Billy went back to the house, saddled and bridled the best black horse the master had, put on the best suit of clothes he could find and, wearing his belt, he rode off to the fight.

When Billy got to the castle, he saw the princess with the entire court around her. He thought he had never seen anyone so beautiful. The knight who was to fight the dragon was there too, walking up and down on the lawn, with three men carrying his sword, and everyone looking at him.

But when the fiery dragon came up, with twelve heads on him and every mouth spitting fire, and let out twelve roars, the knight ran away and hid. The princess asked if there was no one there to save her from the dragon. No one stirred.

Then Billy stepped out of the crowd, swung his stick over his head three times, and went at the dragon with his sword. After a terrible fight entirely, the dragon lay dead.

Everyone gathered around to find out who the stranger was. Billy jumped on his horse. As he was getting away, the princess pulled off one of his shoes.

The knight came out of hiding, cut off the heads of the dragon, and brought them to the king, saying it was he in disguise who had killed the dragon. But when the princess tried the shoe on him, it didn't fit. And she said she would marry no one but the man whose foot was a perfect fit for the shoe.

When Billy got home, he changed his clothes again, put the horse in the stable, and got the cattle home before the master returned.

The king proclaimed that on a certain day, the princess would try the shoe on all the men who came to the castle.

When the day arrived, Billy was in the orchard with the cows, and a crowd passed by. The people stopped to ask Billy if he wasn't going to the castle.

"What would the likes of me be doing there?" Billy replied.

After the others were gone, an old man dressed in rags passed by. Billy stopped him and asked him to swap clothes. At first the old man thought Billy was making fun of him, but when he saw that Billy was serious they swapped clothes, only Billy kept his belt.

Off to the castle went Billy. When he got there he found all the young men in a great commotion trying on the shoe. But the shoe fit none of them. The princess was about to give up in despair, when a ragged-looking lad, who was Billy, elbowed his way through and asked, "Let me try it on. Maybe the shoe will fit me."

The people laughed at the sight of him, but the princess called out, "Come and try."

Billy went up amidst the laughter, and what would you have of it—the shoe fit as nicely as if it had been made for him. So the princess claimed Billy as her husband. Then Billy confessed that it was he who had killed the fiery dragon.

And when Billy was dressed up in a fine silk suit, trimmed with gold and silver, everyone said that they had never seen such a handsome fellow.

Billy and the princess were married. The wedding lasted nine days, nine hours, nine minutes, nine half minutes, and nine quarter minutes.

And they lived happy and well from that day to this.